ORCHARD BOOKS

First published in the US in 2015 by Little, Brown and Company
This edition first published in the UK in 2018 by The Watts Publishing Group

1 3 5 7 9 10 8 6 4 2

A CIP catalogue record for this book is available from the British Library.

ISBN 978 1 40835 242 7

Printed and bound in China

FSC
www.fsc.org

MIX
Paper from
responsible sources
FSC® C104740

Orchard Books
An imprint of Hachette Children's Group
Part of The Watts Publishing Group Limited
Carmelite House
50 Victoria Embankment
London EC4Y 0DZ

An Hachette UK Company
www.hachette.co.uk

www.hachettechildrens.co.uk

WE LIKE SPIKE!

by Jennifer Fox

ORCHARD

Look for these words when you read this book. Can you spot them all?

dragon

breath

heroes

gem

What is purple and green and came from a tiny egg?

It is our friend Spike!

He is a dragon.

Spike is not big or scary like other dragons.

He is little and cute.

He is a great friend
and a super assistant.

Spike uses his magic fire breath to send scrolls.

He is always ready to help.

Spike works really hard.

He also knows how to have fun!

Spike likes to read comic books.

His favourite heroes
are the Power Ponies.

He likes to laugh and
can be very silly!

Spike is a
brilliant friend.

24

Spike loves eating gems.

Spike bakes yummy gem cakes.

Most of the gems do not
end up in the cake.
They end up in his belly!

Spike is not a pony,
but he is family.

We like Spike!

Find out what makes Spike
the dragon such a great friend –
not only to Twilight Sparkle,
Rainbow Dash, Fluttershy, Rarity,
Applejack and Pinkie Pie, but
to all the ponies in Ponyville!

FSC

£3.99

ISBN 978-1-40835-242-7

9 781408 352427

WWW.MYLITTLEPONY.COM

MEET
THE PONIES OF
PONYVILLE